This Book Is Dedicated To

Elizabeth C Ray

1/16/69 -1/16/69

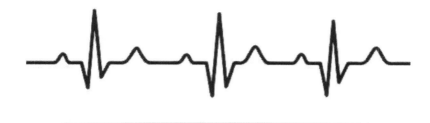

Heart Condition

T E Williams

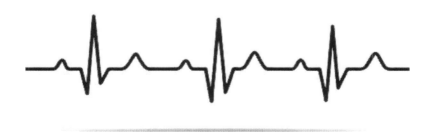

Special Thanks To

Mom & Dad

T E Williams

Chapter 1

Maya McMillan unsheathed her bow from its sleeve and slid it along the rosin stone to powder its soft horse hair. She had played the cello since 3rd grade orchestra, but now played when she was feeling somber. The large awkward instrument loyally resting in her den had become therapeutic like lunch with an old friend.

It was late evening and Maya's lack of an appetite coincided with her melancholy day, so she made a simple dinner salad and retreated to the den. She'd met with three clients in her caseload earlier, each case more depressing than the next, and was forced to violate a 'no show' which automatically meant a warrant had to be issued. She didn't usually bring the rigors of her day home, but the case of Jack King whom she thought she had been positively affecting had Maya discouraged.

Jack King's case she felt, had been misguided and handled poorly by two other parole officers who shoved it along without care. He had been unfairly tried with poor representation for the past year, and the previous handlers of his case seemed uncaring and were due to retire. Jack King had shown up regularly to her mandatory visits, presented with optimistic goals, had clean urine specimens and made tremendous strides returning to society.

She'd become accustomed to hearing good reports from his employer at Unisys and he had reconnected with his estranged wife. It was quite disturbing when she didn't see him walk through her office door and her cello was just the welcome mat needed when she got home.

She pondered about Jack King rosining her long bow, but as she began tuning the cello he faded into oblivion. The sounds of the poignant tones took her mind in another direction. There she was, her mind flashing back to the 3rd grade drifting further in the past, further back with every ominous note; flashback to the day Harmony had come into the world...

"Maya McMillan?" the principal called over the PA system, "Please gather your things and report to my office." Surprised, she rose from her desk grabbing her cello. When Maya arrived, the principal's secretary informed her that she needed to sign out and go home. There had been an emergency. Maya wondered in the chilled November air walking the two blocks home what could have happened. Her mother was pregnant but not due for another two months. She dismissed the thought. Her father was in the Army, and she knew that her mother would have come herself if something had happened to him. He separated from the family shortly after the pregnancy and though he wrote Maya often, he was not able to call because their phone service was disconnected.

As she reached home, she heard wailing from inside the house. Maya dropped her cello ascending the porch steps, her gloves waving from her coat sleeves in the wind and her hood flying off her head to find out what was happening. Maya opened the door and tore up the stairs to see her mother lying on her bed delivering the baby, alone.

The scene was unforgettable, even for an eight year old, and all Maya could do was go hold her mother's hand. No one else was in the house and she felt she couldn't leave her. She hoped a neighbor had heard the commotion and called an ambulance and prayed someone would be coming soon! As fluids and blood discharged from her mother's weakened body, she looked to Maya in anguish with begging eyes travailing then attempted to push, thrusting her upper body forward, when suddenly, her mother fell backwards onto the pillows with her eyes closed.

There was no sound. Maya cried, "Mommy!" She squeezed her hand and felt her tear-filled sweaty face, but there was no response. Maya ran to the bathroom to wet a cloth then returned to clean her mother's face when she realized the baby wasn't crying at all like the programs on television. Her attention was averted to her mother's legs and the poor child tried her best to wipe up the river of blood from the hemorrhage which took her mother's life.

Maya returned to the bathroom 4 times wetting the washcloth with her tiny hands attempting to clean up when finally she noticed the sewing shears by her mother's machine. She went over to grab them and slowly walked back to the baby who was completely still. She gently moved the infant to the side cutting the very middle of the umbilical cord. Maya began to pray. "God please take this baby, it tried but it couldn't do it!" She said looking up wiping her ample tears. Maya reached down at the foot of her mother's bed grabbing sales circulars and newspaper wrapping the tiny baby up placing it in the waste basket along with the massive afterbirth.

She returned to her mother's side. "...And please take care of Mommy!" She said picking up the cloth wiping her mother's neck. She put her ear to her heart and scooped up her forearm as she had seen on television many times, but there was no reaction. Just then Maya heard sirens and voices, and activity could also be heard outside.

As uniformed paramedics darted up the stairs they viewed the sad scene. "Oh no!" one of the men exclaimed covering his mouth while others brushed pass to attend to them. A woman scooped Maya up into her arms removing her to the hall. They checked for vitals and attempted CPR but they were too late. Gwen was gone.

In the hall, Maya saw that it was her neighbor, Ms. Takini who cried holding her. "It was me who called the school, Maya, are you okay? I'm so sorry baby!" Maya cried, "Mommy died today. She don't got no heartbeat." The paramedic immediately rushed out of the room into the hall, "Honey...where's the baby?" Maya slumped down from Ms. Takini's arms walking over to the wastebasket pointing with a sad look, "I tried to keep it, but it wasn't crying!" She began to wail. Ms. Takini took Maya out of the room and the paramedics began the daunting task of attending to the baby.

Moments after the gruesome removal, gasping was all that was heard; then deafening silence. Maya rested on Ms. Takini's bosom feeling completely helpless when all of a sudden, "We got her back! We got her back!" a female paramedic screamed clearing the baby's airway as the baby made her earthly presence known by crying loud enough for Ms. Takini and Maya to hear!

They started an IV on her, rushing both patients out on one gurney. Ms. Takini comforted Maya wishing she'd stayed with Gwen instead of going to her own home to call the school and ambulance. When they heard the baby crying Maya jumped down running to the gurney. "It's okay! Thank you God! It's okay!" She joyfully yelled. The paramedic said, "She's a girl sweetie, you have a baby sister!" Maya looked at her cello case abandoned on the porch. "Her name is Harmony!"

Chapter 2

In present time, Maya strummed the bow against the strings crying softly playing a solemn tune in the quiet candlelit den just off the living room. She began playing Gwen's favorite, *Come By Here*, visualizing the day vividly in her mind moment by moment. She thought of Ms. Takini, who officially adopted the girls due to Gerald's military status.

Ms. Takini was buried last year. She had been the strong woman who raised them along with two sons, which Maya and Harmony lovingly considered their brothers. They were now 33 and 25, and Bill and Dominick were in their 40's. Maya had only communicated with them through social media now.

Harmony had a rough road due to lack of oxygen at birth and she also had a heart murmur. She had several heart surgeries and finally required a heart transplant which was miraculously accepted by her fragile body after a failed first transplant. Harmony remained in the hospital for months.

Ms. Takini petitioned the court for both girls to have a permanent home with her after visiting the hospital every day with Maya. The military funded Gwen's funeral but Gerald, their father relinquished custodial rights returning to Darby in Italy. He had seen very little of the girls through their childhood, but he provided Army allotment funds to contribute to their care. Dear Ms. Takini had treated the girls as her own children through the years until she died from complications of a heart attack.

Maya's seemingly exaggerated vibrato along the vertical strings was indicative of her deep contemplation of that fateful day. When the song ended, she took her sleeve and wiped her face. She began to play a cheerful tune, *Wood Splitter Fanfare* to help change her bleak mood in anticipation of Harmony's arrival from work at Burlington Coat Factory.

The ladies lived in an elegant 2 bedroom 2 bath loft in down town Trenton overtop a barista and two male tenants occupied separate dwellings on the second floor. The smell of ground coffee wafted through the building. Maya and Harmony had access to the roof which boasted a beautiful rooftop garden topiary; mint, basil, sundried tomatoes, bell peppers and fresh oregano naturally grew plentiful in the June sunshine. Maya always maintained enough growth for Chris and Jobie, the downstairs tenants and for the barista owner, Jacque, to barter for whatever it was that the ladies needed. Harmony owned a Yorkshire Terrier, Salope, which means *slut* in French. Jobie and Chris kept cats. The women each had their own tastes in decor which complemented the cozy unit.

Maya was reserved, ambitious and private, but Harmony was more worldly and outspoken. Maya believed, much like Ms. Takini, each being is responsible for the energy and contributions they bring to society; Goodwill tidings bring good, and she believed in humanity's dedication to save itself by doing what needs to be done to make the planet safer and livable for our children. She donated blood when she could, fought for civil rights, reasonable re-entry guidelines for offenders, fair wages and was an active member on the Parole Board.

17

She witnessed how the village collaborated responsibly to raise them, and it took a profound effect on her social outlook. Maya McMillan was a problem solver.

Harmony McMillan's platform was more devil-may-care; to top her life experiences, one after another by taking risks. All her life she had been told she had to sit it out due to her many developmental limitations. She was told she was too small, too weak, needed help; she was used to portable breathing machines, endless allergy meds and an inhaler she carried on her person. She never used her illnesses as a crutch to present herself as weak or needy. In adulthood, Harmony did everything she possibly could with the encouragement of her sister.

Her underdeveloped lungs finally outgrew all the apparatus and she thrived over the years in the loving care of Ms. Takini. She had a host of sexy tattoos, piercings and hairstyles, and she listened to rap music. She'd walk around with her ear buds in moving her head in a rhythmic way to the beat and she even knew how to rap.

It was not important to her what anyone thought about her except Maya.

The ladies resembled their mother in stature which was a little over 5'4", but they dressed very differently. Maya wore stylish professional dresses from Dress Barn always with a blazer even at home, and Harmony wore colorful yet tasteful clothing which required no dry cleaning.

Maya was in the Reserves so she would occasionally be called away to serve. Her fiancé was in the Army stationed in Texas, but was due for discharge. Harmony rose through the ranks in Retail to become Assistant Manager and was considering the course offered through them in Theft Prevention. Harmony worked a 40-hour work week and was exhausted upon reaching home.

"Hey, I'm home!" she said locking the door. When she didn't receive a reply she walked through the spacious loft. "Maya?" She called entering the den to see her bob swinging forward. She silently lifted her head to reveal her teary eyes. "Hi sweetie", she replied clearing her throat, "...you hungry?"

Maya got up tossing her bob placing the cello on its base. "I made a dinner salad." Harmony knew when her sister played, she needed the comfort and solitude it offered and was surprised to hear she had prepared the food. "Yeah, sure, let's eat on the roof, I'll get the bread." The rooftop garden held a small round table, seating for four. The centerpiece was one of the mint plants with other flowering plants around it. It was the perfect day for outdoor dining. The two of them ate silently as the sun was setting. Very little could be heard on the street below other than the whizzing traffic and horns blowing occasionally.

Harmony decided not to initiate conversation with Maya, who was taking small bites of the salad scraping the tines of the fork upside down into her mouth. Harmony sat spinning the homemade bottle of ginger dressing until she finally broke the ice. "You okay?" She asked with half a boiled egg in her cheek causing a protrusion which made her profile look like a chipmunk's.

"Yeah..." Maya answered, "I seasoned that grilled chicken earlier so the flavor..." "You want to talk about it?" Harmony cut her off placing her hand on her sister's. "Harmony, I just get like this every so often when I have to leave you for Service, that's all. I just hate leaving you." Maya offered.

"I could tell it was something. You don't play unless your mind is mush and your heart is full!" Harmony said, softly, assuming Maya's statement was truth, "I love your dedication to your music, and you are the most selfless person I know! Don't worry about me. You know I'll be fine." Maya's expression hadn't changed. She looked at Harmony hearing the words, but had lied. She kept seeing the vision of her as a baby wrapped up in black, white and red; then in hospital in the plastic enclosure with tubes and wires. Harmony still had the mark in her neck from where they removed the largest tube. She finally smiled, "I know you can take care of yourself I just do it better!"

Their time alone was the only occasion Harmony didn't stick her ear buds in. She always wanted to make sure Maya had her full attention, especially when she was due for departure. She understood that they only had each other and their relationship was vital to their legacy. She was Maya's heart, and she must make sure that heart is not broken. Maya tried not to be too overprotective. She gave her gentle guidance and the benefit of her own experiences. Every accolade had been through Maya's example or prompting, and she let her live her own life, but when Harmony wanted to join the Peace Corp she respected her spirit, but discouraged traveling too far. Maya had always given good advice and Harmony knew she had her best interest. She reminded her that she must consider her heart in all decisions. Maya's allegiance to Harmony's health and well being was uncommonly dedicated.

Ms. Takini had Maya write in a journal as a child which she continued throughout her lifetime. She kept it under lock and key by her nightstand. On days like this, Maya would let out her angst via her cello or her journal.

"Where will you be going this time?" Harmony asked. "Stateside. Don't worry, not too far. It'll just be you and Salope." She answered throwing a chunk of the chicken to the dog, who gobbled it looking up with begging eyes. "I'll be back in two weeks." Harmony picked up her wine glass to offer a toast, *"Mi Corazon!"*

Chapter 3

Maya arrived at the Parole Office for her last day before deployment. She took the colorful post stickies and began to mark each file for her staff, keeping things in simple order for them to follow. She came across the file for Jack King and put it to the side contemplating the directive in her job description which indicated the client must make efforts to maintain communication with the Officer.

She still hadn't received a call or message informing of his effort to. Maya tried to make a reasonable breakdown of the directive and how the words can be justified by her reaching out instead. She knew the time limit for pulling the warrant for his arrest was approaching and she was deeply concerned. What happened? She'd violated some within a day, but her hesitation stemmed from his case being neglected for a time and she didn't want to be the caboose on his railroad track back to prison.

Maya decided to call Unisys to speak with his employer one more time. When she called asking the supervisor if he had yet reported, she was informed that he was hospitalized, but the supervisor couldn't give more information.

Maya considered phoning to recall the warrant, but decided to first call local hospitals to verify Jack King had indeed been admitted. It was time consuming, but she'd already dealt with all the other cases so decided to take the time to make the calls. It took quite some time, but found out he was in fact at the Cardiac Care Unit at Cooper in Camden. She was saddened by the news and it pulled at her heartstrings. Maya had learned much about the human heart dealing with Harmony, and her empathy prompted her to pay Jack King a visit. Maya hated hospitals, but she was compelled to go.

She moved appointments around on the calendar, recalled Jack's warrant, said her goodbyes to her coworkers and hit the highway. Maya arrived at the gift shop at Cooper to pick up a card and gift for him and found that he had been transferred to a regular room.

"Hello Jack, how're you feeling today?" Maya asked entering. He was lying to the side with his chest exposed, taped monitors and tubes running down the middle of it. "Hey Miss McMillan, I'm glad you came. I was hoping I didn't get violated for not showing up." Jack managed to say between labored breaths. He smiled with relief, "I had no way to let you know." Maya walked over and handed him his card placing the gift bag on the nightstand. The machines beeped and recorded the data on electronic monitors as a nurse entered to check them.

"You had a heart attack?" Maya asked. "Angina" the nurse offered, "...But if Mr. King doesn't slow down he will." Jack smirked at her returning his gaze to Maya. "I just had a scare." Maya looked seriously at Jack. "Jack I'm happy you made it to the hospital, and I did issue a warrant, but I rescinded it. What can I do for you?" Jack was really surprised at her visit, let alone the card, gift and the offer.

"Miss McMillan just the thought of you coming here to see me is enough. If it weren't for me gambling, I probably would have been at home alone. They told me the stress brought this on. I'm from a big family and nobody's come yet." He admitted. "I'm glad I did then. Jack the nurse is right. The stress will give you a heart attack and it's time for some serious lifestyle changes dude. My sister Harmony was born with a murmur. She had to have a transplant as a baby." She revealed against yet another directive in her manual regarding disclosing her private life to clients. Maya made a mental note. "You get some rest. We'll meet when you're better."

When Maya left the hospital she wrapped up some loose ends at home, fed Salope, and left a love note for Harmony:

> *Dear Harmony,*
>
> *Fed your mutt! Don't forget the tomatoes! I love you!*
>
> *Mi Corazon,*
>
> *Maya*

When Harmony got home from her shift, she knew Maya had gone away and saw the note. She took Salope up to the rooftop to do his business and stood waiting holding the note. She felt her usual sense of foreboding and sighed. "She's gone again, Salope. Lord, please keep her safe." She uttered petting her. She put her ear buds in skipping down the steps back into the kitchen when her phone vibrated. On the line was Keila, her good friend. "Hey Sis, want to go get a drink?" Keila said happily. "Sure, got nothing else going on. Who's driving?" Harmony asked, not willing to sacrifice a good invite. "I'll drive. I'm already here."

Harmony buzzed Keila upstairs and unlocked the door. Keila exited the elevator and went into the loft holding a cup of coffee from Jacque's place. "You know I can't resist his espresso!" She said grasping the cup with two hands. "I can't drink hot stuff in the summer, you know that." Harmony said holding up two outfits on hangers. "Which? Tangerine or plum?"

"The plum" Keila answered honestly. "We have pictures of you in the tangerine at Dave & Buster's." "Yeah, we do…" said Harmony tossing the tangerine jumper onto her bed covering Salope. She slid into the plum dress and jelled down the edges of her short cropped hair in the mirror. Keila held up black sandals for her to see and placed them in front of Harmony. The ladies posed in the mirror with their arms around one another smiling. "We look great!" Keila said. They left the loft and were off to Smokehouse for drinks.

Harmony ordered Long Beach iced tea for them and Keila ordered wings with garlic barbecue sauce, which were especially good. The establishment held an upscale feel and the customers were the working class. The ladies enjoyed going on karaoke night, and never missed a chance to enter their names.

After a few more drinks Keila noticed that they had a few admirers eyeing them after singing *I'm Every Woman* and *Girls Just Wanna Have Fun*, their standard. The two short gentlemen came over and introduced themselves as James and Tyree, offering to buy drinks, but Keila said they'd had drinks, but thanked them. Harmony insisted that they sit. James asked Keila, "What do you guys do, sing for a living?" Keila entertained the question by calling his bluff. "Yeah, you an agent?"

James didn't find it so amusing. Harmony recovered, "Excuse her, she's normally really nice! I'm in Retail and Keila's at Unisys. What do you do?" Tyree who was looking at Harmony's legs looked up to see the question was directed at him. "I work at WalMart! So I guess I'm in Retail too!" They all laughed. Tyree looked as if it was his first time officially in a bar. He joined in the laughter so the ladies took it as a sign he was the good humor type. James said, "I drive a forklift for Amazon. This is my only day off."

"I think that's admirable" Keila said. "...And manly!" Keila stretched her eyes and leaned in toward James. "How old are you?" Harmony asked Tyree. He said boldly, "21!" Harmony nodded. It wasn't taking off as Tyree had hoped and he got up from the table and marched away. James' name was called from the karaoke list and the ladies looked at him surprised. "Go! Go!" Keila shouted, excited to see him do his thing.

James had an old soul. He looked up from the mic softly harmonizing *Love and Hapiness*, and when the beat came in, he rocked his short body back and forth with rhythm and Keila couldn't take her eyes off him! The crowd began snapping their fingers dancing in the small bar. It was quite impressive. They had a great night out and James ended up taking Keila home. She tossed Harmony the keys promising to be there to pick it up in the morning.

After James and Keila left, Harmony nursed her drink looking around at the others dancing and enjoying the music. Tyree walked slowly back over to her booth, "Can we...begin again?" he said coyly. Harmony smiled at him. "Have a seat" she offered. "Hi, I'm Tyree, people call me Junie. I'm 21 and my mother says I'm wise beyond my years. I work at WalMart and I'm studying Web Design at the Art Institute. I'm not shy and don't mind approaching beautiful women who tend dismiss me."

Harmony listened intently. "Well, Junie, it's nice to make your acquaintance. My name is Harmony McMillan, I'm 25. I work at Burlington Coat Factory. I don't have a boyfriend, but have a lot of male friends. I'm drinking Long Beach iced tea in a pretty glass..." she said giggling hinting for him to buy her a drink. Tyree got up went to the bar and ordered her drink and one for him, placing the long stemmed glass in front of her on its napkin.

"Thank you." she said, "For the record, I actually didn't imply anything, you inferred from my reaction that I wouldn't be interested. You should have kept the confidence it took to approach me. I didn't mean to run you off." Tyree shifted in the seat. "You know Harmony, you're right. It's been something I've dealt with in my experience. I assume she's not interested because I'm young, but I really have no issues with my age, I'm not ashamed. I know more than most just from observing before I speak." Harmony smiled wide. "Now that's a mature, confident man. Let's not make any assumptions from now on." She suggested.

Just then, the karaoke host asked if anyone else wanted to sing. Harmony walked over and took the mic whispering to the host. As the music started, she closed her eyes in the spotlight opening them in time for the first note, *What You Won't Do For Love*, Bobby Caldwell. When the part of the song came that says 'you've tried everything but you don't give up', Harmony walked over to Tyree and belted with her head back, 'In my world, only you, make me do for love what I would not do...' he sat watching her with a sense of humility on the part that says, 'I came back to let you know, got a thing for you and I can't let go', he joined in.

Chapter 4

About a week later, Harmony was at work sifting through the markdown list with a pink highlighter. "Sheena, please do the markdowns in the Plus Department." She ordered. Sheena was the laziest worker in the store and would rather have the Dressing Room post because very few people tried on clothes, and she hated customer interaction. She rolled her eyes and took the clipboard. "Nyeem, you take the Shoe Department, and Cho, you got Young Miss. I'll do the Children's Department myself."

When Harmony got engrossed in marking down the prices in red she was distracted by the nagging presence of someone standing nearby. Naturally she looked up smiling assuming it was a customer but as she did, the person disappeared. She went back to her work and shrugged it off thinking it may have been a child playing in the display rack. A couple of minutes later she looked up again, but no one was there.

Harmony glanced at her watch and called for Sheena and Cho to go on break. She and Nyeem would take the second lunch. Nyeem had finished his work in the Shoe Department and came to Harmony for more markdowns. "Nyeem, did you ever get the feeling you were being watched?" she asked. "I hope they're looking 'cause I paid a lot for this outfit!" he said with a flourish. Harmony laughed and handed him the clipboard of the markdowns for the Men's Department.

Nyeem was a handsome, groomed, well read gentleman; a real GQ eligible bachelor with many female callers. There was an endless line of Nyeem fans waiting in line to be his plus-one to the many club openings, art exhibits and sporting events he attended. He had no children and was as outspoken and risqué as Harmony was with no regrets. The two enjoyed working with one another, and the manager put them on work schedule together often because they were the two hardest workers.

When the Children's Department was finished, Harmony took her break with Nyeem while the others took to the floor. They warmed their food and sat in the break room quietly speaking about the karaoke at Smokehouse and Tyree approaching her, and how she really liked him. Nyeem spoke of his upcoming trip to Atlanta which he was looking forward to. He had requested two weeks off, and Harmony was preparing herself for the double workload she'd have to pull due to his absence.

She'd done it before. He took a trip to Amsterdam the previous year and was gone a month. Nyeem and Keila were the only two she invited over for cocktails and Maya got along with both. They were a mish mosh of different personalities and the energy they gave was always positive and fun. Harmony and Maya were selective with whom they had over. They each knew of Harmony's health issues and of Maya's job.

"You got your agenda for your trip all in place Nyeem?" Harmony asked. "Not really! I'm going to be spontaneous and free. I'm going to take it as it comes. I got my hotel and flight booked. Whatever happens happens!" He said tossing his tie. "When's Maya due back?" Harmony spooned her yogurt. "July 3rd, just in time for

Independence; I'm considering surprising her with a little get together. She's usually wiped out after Service though. You coming?" She asked. "Of course! I wouldn't miss it!" Nyeem said.

The markdowns were done by the evening and upon the store closing Sharon the Manager counted out the register receipts. Each employee was let out of the store as they clocked out and Harmony and Nyeem checked the store for anyone lingering. The three pulled down the heavy metal outer gate and walked to their cars. There was a car sitting aloof in an odd spot Harmony noticed and casually looked to see if there was an occupant but the driver's seat was reclined. She pulled out behind the others and drove to the loft tired from a long day.

When she got home she allowed Salope to relieve herself and tended to Maya's tomatoes with the water hose. Harmony went down to shower and clicked her music on while warming up leftover chicken fried rice. She headed to her room with her ear buds in and gobbled up the food falling asleep on top of her fluffy comforter. Harmony fell into a deep sleep too tired to answer the text from Tyree.

Harmony awoke at 8:00am with Salope licking her toes. Snatching one of the buds out she heard the sound of the garbage truck outside and it caused her to growl. She sat up realizing that it hadn't been taken out. She jumped up urgently and threw on her satin robe running to the kitchen to retrieve the trash.

She ran down just in time to greet the truck collectors who wore the city green and orange attire. They gazed at her exposed legs through the bathrobe opening. One of them donning a black du rag took the trash out of her hand, "I got it" he said. No cat calls. The truck lingered in the front as they had to collect all Jacque's business garbage.

She trotted back into the house smoothing her short tapered hair closing the robe on the way. She closed her door then replaced the liner in the can when Harmony stopped in her tracks. She instinctively felt something was amiss looking around noticing the plate on the counter. Walking back into her room she looked for the plate she thought was left on her nightstand but it was gone. Harmony chalked it up to pure exhaustion and went on with her day. She put on her workout gear and ankle weights and put her ear buds in heading for a run through town. She ran through Warren Street, down Lafayette past the War Memorial, up Barrack Street to Willow, then Bank Street all the way to Perry, then Stockton Street to Mill Hill Park stopping to stretch, then back home to Warren.

When Harmony walked in to greet Jacque he was at his busiest serving customers and she waved then put her 'hang loose' sign to her ear basically saying she'd call him later. She'd gathered some tomatoes for him and wanted to exchange for 2 lbs of his best brew for Keila.

She got into the elevator and hit 3, but the doors hesitated so she held the railing stretching her foot to her inner thigh with her arms straight out. Harmony reached the loft grabbing a towel to cool her neck and a bottle of water out of the refrigerator. She eyed the plate on the counter again laughing for not remembering returning it to the kitchen the previous night. She showered, dressed and boiled two eggs then went to the rooftop to grab the basket of tomatoes she'd gathered for Jacque when she heard the buzzer. It was Keila coming to pick up her car after the long week.

"Girl, James may be short, but he ain't short everywhere!" She jested entering. "You didn't!" Harmony chastised. Keila was not normally promiscuous, but she hadn't dated in a while and Harmony was always the first to hear of her sexual escapades. "I had this leg over his shoulder and..." Harmony waved her hand, "TMI Keila, TMI!" They sat giggling.

"Tyree turned out to be a surprise too. He bought drinks, we talked. I like him." Harmony admitted. "He's a student; I think I'm attracted to his good nature and intellect." "But they're so...short! I mean, for men. I've never dated a short guy! You know how shallow I can be girl!" Keila confessed. "We're not perfect! You never know what package God has for you until you open it, and besides, they were still the best looking two in the place that evening". Harmony observed. "Listen, I have to run these tomatoes and herbs down to Jacque, want to come?"

"Sure" Keila said following her, "I could use a latte." Harmony grabbed her keys and started for the elevator. When it opened on the 1st Floor, both Chris and Jobie were entering with another gentleman all carrying cumbersome packages. "Hey fellas! You guys usually skip up the stairs, but I can see why that's not possible." Harmony said.

Jobie answered, "Hey li'l sis, yeah, we went to the farmer's market over at Mill Hill. They have the organic veggies and great wine. I got you guys some Sangria." Jobie nodded at Chris to hand it to Harmony, but his hands were full too, so the guy who was unfamiliar to the ladies grabbed the wine with his free hand interceding for the two, but never said a word. Harmony and Keila thanked them and exited the elevator, but Harmony turned.

"Maya has some tomatoes for you by the way." Harmony said. "Thanks Harmony. I'll come get them later." Keila noticed that when Chris said it, he had a strange look on his face behind the brown grocery bag handle. He was looking back and forth from the odd fellow to the ladies. She didn't mention it to Harmony because she figured they must've had a laugh at their expense or a private joke among them. "They seem nice. Are they gay?" She asked Harmony. "I don't think so Keila. You forget James that quickly?" Harmony asked sarcastically. "No, I was just wondering...there are only two apartments up there right?" Keila asked. "Yeah, but they pretty much do things together. Good dudes." Harmony answered.

They saw Jacque seated in a corner with his apron around his neck. "Busy day huh, Jacque? Here you go. Maya said to make sure you got this basket." Jacque stood to greet the ladies and grabbed the basket. "Thanks love, sweet of her. Ahhh! Sangria, from Jobie and Chris, huh? I got some too. You gals want some coffee? "I'll take a French vanilla cappuccino and a scone please!" Keila requested grinning. Harmony's eyes rolled. "No thanks love, but I'd love some ground coffee." Jacque got up to fill their order bagging the coffee.

"He's hot!" Keila whispered. "Shut up Keila!" Harmony said laughing.

Chapter 5

Harmony finally had a much needed day off and was cleaning the loft, vacuuming her room, dusting the furniture and watering the plants. She flopped down in the den looking at the engraved cello resting on its base thinking of Maya. She decided she'd better shop for the get together because Maya was due home soon. Harmony tried thinking of something Maya needed that she could give as a gift. She wasn't hard to shop for and had many interests, but she was hard pressed to think of something Maya wouldn't purchase for herself.

She looked in Maya's bathroom. There were soaps and creams, Mary Kay items, several mirrors and hair ties. She had bath sheets in every color and several loofahs, a pumice stone, different relaxation fragrances for the aromatic decanter and many, many candles. When Harmony slid the shower door she saw Maya's journal keychain dangling from the shower head and thought, "Dare I?" She slid the shower door closed, crept into Maya's room and felt beside her bed for the journal. When Harmony found the huge journal, she noticed two others and reached for them as well. The key was universal, and she decided to sneak a peek at the first. She didn't know what force was behind it. She wasn't curious by nature and a tinge of guilt crossed her mind, but she felt she was already committed and there was no threat of getting caught, so continued.

When Harmony began reading the first few pages of the first journal her heart began to pound. It was kind of a manifesto about the guilt Maya felt for years as a child dealing with the stigma surrounding Harmony's birth; how she was tossed into the trash by her own sister and how she's still tormented by it but intends to take it to her grave.

Harmony knew she was not born in a hospital. She knew she had to be revived by paramedics and that their mother died bringing her into the world. She had heard the story countless times from Maya, Ms. Takini and her father. She was now learning about being tossed in the garbage.

The morbid scene was described vividly by Maya in the faded journal, and the torment she felt was expressly apparent as Harmony read line after line and became more and more uncomfortable. She understood now that Maya not only went to great lengths to conceal her deeply rooted feelings of guilt from her, but that her sister had not gotten over the loss of their mother and blamed her for her death.

Tears streaming down her face, she closed and locked the journal, eyeing the second. This book was much thicker and began as a more recent reflection of the same story. Not much changed except it was clear it was written by Maya as an adult. The scene again was described in colorful detail using metaphors that sickened Harmony. Maya's guilt had evolved into resentment for Harmony and included expressions of the hate for their father whom she felt abandoned by, and the bitterness of having to help Harmony through tough times and how she hated the smell of hospitals because of it.

She read how Maya knew as much about the human heart as any physician, but purposely chose another avocation so she wouldn't fail.

Maya expressed feelings of being an under-achiever. Harmony read angry, bitter, hate-filled words attached to sacrifice and diminished goals and settling in her life carrying the *baggage* that is Harmony McMillan. She also read how Maya intentionally chose to say *yes* to her fiancé because his Army life was almost over and she would finally be able to again cut the proverbial umbilical cord symbolically connected to Harmony.

She continued to read until the end then angrily slammed the second book closed locking it. Her heart sunk anxiously reaching for the third volume and as she stuck the key in she heard Salope scratching at the rooftop entrance door to be let in. An hour had passed and it was time for her to eat. Harmony stomped out of Maya's room and snatched the door open to let the dog in.

When she attempted to close it behind her, someone stuck a foot in to prevent it! Harmony screamed but her mouth was forcefully covered and she passed out from the chloroform tainted rag placed over it. She fell forward and was dragged to the living room, the dead weight of her thrown to the floor. Harmony was gagged, tied up and duct taped to an armchair. Salope barked and barked, but her annoying nuisance was quelled when the man muffled her and broke the poor dog's neck.

Hours later Harmony came out of her daze wondering what had happened. Her head was spinning and her eyes were blurry. She realized she was gagged and tied when she wriggled to move and tried to speak. Her eyes darted around, the tape tightly wrapped around her face, she became panicked. As her vision slowly returned, she focused enough to see the silhouette of a thin Black man seated before her. He stood and walked over leaning to meet her face with his. She could see only his army fatigues and a large blade.

"Hello Harmony" the strange voice said. She tried to place the voice but couldn't. Her heart pounded and tears rolled down as she wriggled to and fro. "...we're going to spend some time together, you and I. Your sister's away. Your girlfriend is not going to call. Your gay ass coworker is dead along with your corny ass neighbors. No one is looking for you. Now you're not a stupid girl, so don't be stupid. I'm going to remove this tape. You scream and I'll kill you. Understand?"

Harmony heavily breathed in an out nodding looking at the knife he held, then back at him. He paused before he made any attempt to remove the gray tape, making sure she understood then snatched it off with force. She winced, but didn't scream. "You have something that I need. I can't afford the time to be on some damn waiting list for another 5 years!" the man said with anger.

"Sir, my vision is blurred. Technically I haven't seen your face! Please let me go...I won't..." she begged, but he put his hand with the blade over her mouth. "Shut up", he said very calmly, relaying to Harmony that this man was not some crazed lunatic, which frightened her all the more. He was not of limited intelligence and he was calculating in his plan to get what he wanted.

"I've been watching you Harmony. I know your routines, where you work, who you chill with, and every inch of this apartment building. I know nobody's coming here for another week, and by then, I will have what I need." The man said. "I don't need anyone interfering with what needs to be done, understand?" Her eyes stretched wide. Harmony could only focus on the shiny blade near her mouth. She hesitated to speak, but her mind was racing as she tried to place recollection of his voice. She was telling the truth about his blurred face; she hadn't gotten her full vision back, but could make out the knife and the camouflage jacket. She did realize she was in her own home and wondered where Salope was.

"What is it that you need that I can give?" She blurted out with tears. The man stood straight up, opening his jacket wide, "Your heart." He suddenly punched her in the side of the head knocking her out cold.

When Harmony came to, she felt the swell of her cheekbone and the pain, but her vision had returned. She was still tied, but the duct tape was not over her mouth. She surveyed the scene. No Salope, but she listened to hear if she was alone. She saw the table was covered in white cloth and a tray table was lined with an assortment of tools and surgical instruments.

A Red Cross organ 'lunchbox' was on the floor opened, a surgical saw sat ominously upright, and a huge metal tub sat next to it. There was also a pick axe and what can only be described as a chest cracker on the floor. Her heart pounded!

Harmony wriggled furiously attempting to find a way to get free. She thrust her body to and fro, side to side all while continuing to listen for subtle noises. When she didn't hear anything, she caused the front of the chair to move up and down off the floor with her body in it. Her feet were duct taped to the chair legs, so she could not stomp. Moving the whole chair up and down was the only way she could make a sound besides yelling, and she didn't want to take that threat lightly.

Again and again she caused the chair to thump, but no one came. Hours had passed, but no one could hear the chair thump. She recalled the man stating that Chris and Jobie were already dead, and because they weren't coming to investigate the noise, she believed him. She cried thinking about them, and thought of

Jacque, Keila and Nyeem. Finally, she thought of what was happening to her and panicked.

"I did not come this far to die now!" She said angrily. She looked around again at the many tools lined up, then tried to hop the chair in that direction, but she was too heavy. She rocked it to see if she could at least fall in the general direction, but it was no use. He had her confined to the sturdiest chair in the place.

Harmony sat thinking of how she could help herself when her early afternoon snoop session invaded her thoughts. "Maya!" she whispered. She no longer cared about what Maya had written in her journal, she needed her sister right now. Blood is amazing! It literally dictates what is actually of value to a person in the darkest of times! A couple of hours ago, she felt betrayed, devalued, disgusted and was feeling like Maya's anchor, but actually, she realized Maya was her life preserver!

She felt the sting of guilt again. Oh how she wished she never saw that journal key! It's all behind her now. Harmony was in real danger and the man had already admitted that he killed for what he wanted. He certainly had demonstrated that he was capable of it. He wanted her heart! He didn't want money. He hadn't expressed any fulfillment of sexual desires or a need to feel dominant. He wanted her heart, but how was this to be accomplished?

Harmony knew what she had to do. She thought about everything he'd said, so she could exploit a weakness, but he didn't seem to have any. He said he knew the building top to bottom. How long had it been under his surveillance? Where did she know him from? Where was he now?

She thought about Maya's military ties due to his dress in the camouflage gear and the army blade he carried, but she quickly ruled that out. Maya always said that her tours didn't net friends because she was never anywhere long enough to make them, and she was very private. She thought of Burlington Coat Factory, but couldn't conclude a connection to it. She thought of James and Tyree, but it just didn't add up. They weren't *streetish*! They were two extremely sensitive guys who were looking for companionship.

Harmony's vision was now fully restored, but she was still afraid to scream. He may be just up on the rooftop garden, and he would hear. Whatever she was going to do, she would have to think fast.

Chapter 6

Maya sat at the airport terminal with her knees over her heavy green duffle waiting for her flight to board. She played Candy Crush until boarding call, excited to be going home. She was feeling underwhelmed because her only post in ½ a month was to guard a National Monument with four other Reservists.

There were times when she had to run drills, stock armor, even cut mountains of potatoes for the Chow Hall. She called it busy work; it was honorable and rewarding. The training was incredible and she felt whatever it was she needed to do to serve, she'd do. A weekend per month was too intense, but a full two weeks per year was fine by her. This post was boring as hell for her, yet she didn't want to view her service as myopic or tenuous. The rewards for serving far outweighed the tasks.

When her flight was called she boarded and thought about what lie ahead. She looked forward to hearing about Harmony's escapades, watching the Thunder Field fireworks from the rooftop, and eating some good pasta. She thought, 'those sundried tomatoes should be perfect!'

Meanwhile, Harmony had managed to tilt the chair backwards to a degree that it could possibly fall. She thrust it back; it came back down. She thrust it back with more force and it toppled backward slowly and it landed flush on the floor again. She cried, frustrated. "Damn it!"

Harmony began to pray, "Lord please! If you get me out of this, I will forever worship you! I promise not to snoop through Maya's things! I promise I will guard my heart! I forgive her for all she wrote! I promise with my broken heart! He's going to kill me!!!"

She stopped and thought. 'He wants my heart. He's got to have some connection to Cooper! How would he even know I'd be compatible? How is he going to know my blood type? And who the hell is he getting to surgically remove it in my living room?'

Then it clicked all at once. 'He's the strange man from the elevator! No wonder Keila had asked if there were only two apartments on the second floor! It's obvious in retrospect! He was not only unfamiliar to us; he was unfamiliar to them too! The guys probably wondered if they were going up and we were headed down, what apartment was HE headed to? Jobie and Chris would have introduced him had he been with them! Oh my God! They were killed then! Otherwise they'd have come up for the tomatoes by now!'

"He should have killed me when he had the chance!" She shouted. Harmony threw her body backward with all her might, but as it finally tilted back far enough, it came down too hard and she hit the back of her head on Maya's cello! She was again knocked out, her head wound bleeding profusely.

Maya entered Jacque's place to the familiar smell of home. She dropped the heavy duffle and greeted him. The place was totally emptied of customers and he was totaling receipts. "Hi buddy! It's so good to be home! How're you? How's my sister?" Jacque's face sunk and he turned his lip up, "I haven't seen her in days. I thought it was odd, but you know Harmony." He said looking quizzically. "Did she give you the tomatoes?" Maya asked, her heart sinking. She knew it was not like Harmony to not be seen at least once a day, and although Jacque is a busy man, she knew she would always pop her head in to say hello. "Come to think of it Maya, I haven't seen Jobie or Chris lately either."

Maya suddenly retreated out of the side door in a panic, "Call 911 Jacque!" She said brandishing her service weapon from its holster holding it high over her head. Jacque was startled but he didn't see any reason to make the call. "I'm sure they're fine Maya I..." Maya held her hand out in authority causing Jacque to stop in his tracks. His Adam's apple shot up and down and he became beet red! Afraid, he quickly ducked down behind his counter grabbing the cordless on the way down nervously depressing the numbers.

Maya placed her back against the wall and crept along it listening for any sound. There were none. She ascended the spiral staircase in the lobby which led to the 2nd Floor elevators and tipped up them like a stealthy ninja. The 2nd

Floor hallway lights were out. She put her ear to Jobie's door, but there was no sound. She felt the door jamb for any signs of tampering then slid along the wall to Chris's door further down the hall. She could hear his cat meowing and could tell by the sound it hadn't been fed. Maya's heart beat fast, but she was skillfully trained and knew she couldn't allow emotions or fear to interfere.

Her boots were laced up tightly. Her eyes were focused. Her mind stayed sharp in the darkness. She ascended the next flight of stairs to her own place. The lights were off in the 3rd Floor hallway as well, which was further confirmation that something was horribly wrong. Maya stood on the side of the door with her back against the wall then felt around the doorknob. She then attempted to peep into the peephole, but it only minimized the view. *'Mi Corazon!'*

Maya hoisted her leg and kicked her own door in to see her sister lying duct taped to the chair with her head hemorrhaging. She quietly ran in and bent to check her pulse which was strong. Harmony was only unconscious. Maya checked every room, but the place was empty. She tipped out of the glass door and ascended the outer staircase to the rooftop garden topiary popping her head up quickly and down again. She saw Salolpe's lifeless body and knew immediately she was gone, but didn't let it distract her.

Maya crept back down the stairs listening cautiously. She still hadn't heard any sirens from the Trenton Police Department and knew what she'd have to do; she had to get herself and her little sister out. She took out her blade and released Harmony from the chair, hoisted her over her shoulder and made her way down the stairs, as far as the 2nd Floor landing when she heard the elevator ascending!

Maya wondered what to do but could not leave Harmony in harm's way. Her superior training kicked in. Before the doors opened, she shot by as if she was doing a true military drill carrying Harmony all the way to the end of the hallway. She unlocked and opened the large window and tossed her into Jacque's dumpster which was filled with bags and half empty coffee cups. She jumped down to the side of it. "This is the 2nd time I've had to throw my bloody sister in the damn trash!" She said through clenched teeth dusting herself off. Maya had no choice! She looked up in time to see a set of Black hands gripping the window sill! She swiftly hopped into the dumpster in one leap closing the lid! She looked through the crack at the top to see Jack King looking far down the alley one way, then the other with the blade in his hand. He was angry. He slammed the window shut so hard that glass could be heard hitting the lid of the dumpster!

Maya stayed as still as possible holding her sister's head in her arms, "Hold on baby!" She said. She didn't know how long Harmony was out, but her pulse was not as strong as it was before. She had to get her help immediately, but her duffle bag and cell phone was left inside!

'Where in the hell is Jacque!? Where are the cops!?' She thought. No sirens could be heard at all, from a distance even! She would have to save them herself. She pulled Harmony up over her shoulder again from a kneeling position but just when she was about to stand, someone kicked the dumpster!

Maya's heart was racing 90 miles per hour! She held the gun toward the lid keeping Harmony as still as she possibly could when she heard, "Police!! I know you're in there! Come out now!!!" A deep authoritative voice shouted! Maya holstered her weapon praising God! "I'm Officer Master Sergeant Maya McMillan! I live here! My sister needs immediate medical attention! We're coming out now! I do have a weapon, but it's holstered now! Are you alone? We're coming out!!! Don't shoot!" Maya hollered back praying to the good Lord that it was not Jack King!

When she slowly opened the lid and peeked, she saw a uniformed officer in the Weaver stance holding his Glock with stiff arms. Maya screamed, "Thank God! Come help fool!" The officer cautiously approached the women with the weapon and observed Harmony's bloody body covered in gray duct tape and coffee grounds. "My partner's with Mr. Miller. He's safe. I called for backup!" He said urgently as he helped her take Harmony out of the dumpster. Finally, the sirens could be heard coming down Perry. "We've got to get her to the hospital! I'm an Officer, it's Jack King! One of my parolees! I'll give a full statement after we make sure my sister's okay!" Maya yelled.

Chapter 7

Harmony McMillan was immediately rushed to the Emergency Department at Capital Health Center in Hopewell in the officer's squad car. Maya accompanied her of course, holding onto her hand gingerly removing the gray duct tape from her hair, her eyes filled with tears. The ambulance had not yet arrived and Maya told him it was his responsibility to make sure he preserved her life pleading their case. In the interim, she filled the officer in on what had taken place once she arrived home from the airport. He taped her statement on an audio recorder while the details were fresh in her mind, Independence Day fireworks displays in the sky everywhere.

As Maya revealed what she knew, she began describing the scene of the loft and realized all the tools and equipment and the Red Cross lunchbox that were all displayed in the living room when it hit her. Flashbacks of her standing in Jack King's hospital room discussing Harmony's heart transplant shot back in her mind. "He was after her heart! King was after Harmony's heart!" She hollered. "He...He has problems with his heart! The guy has heart problems! He needs a transplant!!"

Harmony's pressure was dropping from blood loss and her pulse was weak upon arrival to the ER. The cop hopped out and helped Maya carry her to a gurney. What seemed like 40 doctors and nurses ran out to meet them and they all rushed to keep her heart beating to save her life.

Maya had run alongside the gurney, but they'd finally arrived to a large room with double doors she was not allowed to enter. Maya banged and begged, but she was not allowed entry. The nurses had to physically push her back. She paced the hallway crying in her fatigues, Harmony's blood all over her. All she could do was cry pounding her fists.

She began to pray loudly regardless of the spectators and bystanders watching who had witnessed it all, "God please!" She yelled, "She's all I got! It's all my fault!" Maya looked at the sympathetic faces and began grabbing them one by one. "It's my fault! It's my fault! You don't understand! She's my heart! That's my baby sister! It's all my fault!!!" She yelled banging her palm against her chest. Finally she slumped in a corner removing her service cap smashing her face into it. More nurses came running holding her down administering a shot for her hysteria. They helped her onto her own gurney and two orderlies rolled her to an area behind a curtain.

When she awoke, she had no recollection of the breakdown, just what had happened to Harmony. She furiously depressed the call button. When the male nurse arrived, she calmed. "I need to be with my sister Harmony McMillan, is there an update?" she asked. "Your sister lost a lot of blood. We're doing what we can for her." He said softly. "It doesn't look good. I'm afraid that's the only update I can give."

Maya broke down crying again, and the nurse rushed over to administer yet another sedative into the IV. She didn't fight. She just balled herself up in a knot repeating, "It's all my fault!"

When she woke up two detectives were at her bedside. She wiped her mouth and asked about Harmony. She could tell some hours had passed and need to know the status of everything.

"Hi dear, I'm Detective Haynes, this is Detective Cohen. We heard your recorded statement and just have some follow up questions. First, I want you to know that Harmony's in a coma. She has normal brain activity so she's not brain dead. She suffered a blow to her head and the loss of blood and lack of oxygen to her brain caused her to slip into a coma. She's in ICU. I'm sorry."

"When can I see her? Is King in custody?" Maya asked, but the detective continued without answering.

"I also want to inform you that your neighbors have been identified by their families. They were both found stabbed over 20 times. We think they were killed sometime Friday morning. Another young woman, Keila Henson survived after being stabbed six times in the back. She has over 200 stitches, a collapsed lung and is on a respirator. She was found in a custodial closet just off the 2nd Floor of your building, it's a miracle she survived. She works at Unisys with King." Detective Haynes flipped through his notepad. "Nyeem Jeffers who works with your sister was not considered missing because he was supposed to be away on a trip. His body's been discovered behind Retro Fitness Thursday night. He was stabbed at least 13 times. We believe he was the first victim. Your dog's neck was broken. Jacque Miller's shaken up, but he's fine."

Maya took a deep breath and repeated. "When can I see my sister?" Detective Cohen opened the door and motioned to the nursing staff to approach.

"Ms. McMillan", Detective Haynes began, "King slipped through our fingers. We have some good leads. There was a mountain of evidence left at your building because you surprised him. If you hadn't showed when you did, your sister would not be alive. It's just a matter of time. You were right. He was after your sister's heart. How he intended to have it transplanted into his own chest remains a mystery."

"Damn!"

Chapter 8

Harmony McMillan remained in a comatose state with her older sister never leaving her side. Maya McMillan took a leave of absence from her Parole duties so she could be with Harmony night and day. She cried a lot; prayed a lot. The detectives periodically came to check Harmony's status which was grave, and to update Maya on the investigation.

Through the course of the investigation the trail of evidence Jack King left behind began at Cooper Cardiac Care. He hacked their computer system almost immediately after he learned Harmony's name learning her blood type, her medical history, her allergies and medications, address, employment, insurance information and family history. He stalked her, following her daily movements then killed or tried to kill any potential threat to his plan. He learned Maya would be away by one of her own staff, which gave him the perfect opportunity to plan his diabolical crime.

The ultimate creepy definition 'stalker' fit Jack King's criminal profile. The more the detectives investigated, the stranger his stalker behavior was revealed! They found he was actually dwelling in their building in different rooms of every apartment, including the McMillan's loft. They found he was sleeping under Maya's own bed the day she wrote the farewell note to Harmony and departed! Salope never gave him up; dumb dog was fed special treats and considered King a family member!

King had intentionally left Maya's journal key in her shower for Harmony to find there to distract her. He read them to somehow manipulate to gain better advantage. He *had* been spying from the parking lot of her job and in fact, gone in to see her up close. He *had* moved the plate from Harmony's room to the kitchen. He even followed her on her jogging path actually having had a brief conversation with her at Mill Hill Park that day. The investigation revealed that the trash collectors believed that Jack King was Harmony's significant other! They'd been interacting with him as such for two weeks! Poor Nyeem Jeffers never made it out of the parking lot.

It is so important to be aware of your surroundings and to occasionally break from your routine. Don't discount your gut thinking that you're crazy or exhausted when you find something out of place or not where you originally placed something. Predators are looking for you to slip or forget or doubt yourself.

Don't leave windows cracked or doors unlocked. If two of you live in one dwelling, develop a system that lets the other know that it was you that did something last like unloading the dishwasher or eating the last Twinkie. If you're the first to reach home, check the house; send a simple text if you see the plants have been watered, or the dog's been fed. There are systems for safety to be explored and practiced so when you do encounter a stalker, you're prepared.

These individual incidents seem benign, but if you link all of the odd things that were happening consecutively and present them to yourself on paper, you will begin to connect those dots and may even save your own life.

Furthermore, don't reveal too much about yourself initially. Keep conversations with your friends low. Predators hear key words and latch on to use at a later time. Gender, age, race, religion, social standing, intelligence or looks have no bearing on who falls under the title of 'stalker', so there's no specific type to look for. What they do have in common is persistency.

Using technology to stalk has become prevalent since the 90's, and using public and private information to learn about you is endless. Stalkers will create opportunities to have contact with you. They'll even go through your trash so invest in a document shredder.

Don't waste your emotional energy on beating yourself up if you have been stalked, and don't blame yourself or consider what you could have done. When we know better we do better. It does not translate to inadequacy or insecurity on the victim's part. You don't have to change your entire lifestyle. You do need to be diligent with being aware, taking precautions and not sharing information.

Maya sat at Harmony's bedside pouring out all her guilty feelings from not being able to deal with her birth to leaving her for the last tour. She didn't know whether Harmony could really hear her, but she managed between her tears and grief to explain it all, and felt better afterward.

It was heavy.

For six weeks Maya sat with her waiting for some reaction. She waited for the arrest of Jack King. She didn't attend the funerals of their friends. She didn't work or attend meetings. She had one final contact with Jacque who was traumatized. He required therapy upon learning he was a potential target. He closed his shop and moved away.

Maya had contacted and informed their adoptive brothers who promised to come to visit Harmony at the hospital. Tyree and James had visited bringing flowers introducing themselves as friends. Security was tight on her floor. Keila Henson was just recently released. She would also require therapy of more than one sort.

Maya prayed without ceasing and fasted for a week. She visited St. Michael's on Warren Street and sought religious counseling which was provided two hours per day at no cost. She felt numb, lacked sleep and kept vigil by Harmony who was to be transferred to Morris Hall, a more suitable hospice and rehab. Her fiancé was to arrive within the week for final discharge. She intended to call off the wedding and wanted to tell him face to face. Maya knew she wasn't prepared to have a ceremony after this whole atrocious incident. There were too many variables; will she have to bury her only sister?

Maya returned to the hospital and entered Harmony's room pass Security. She tossed old flowers from the glass vases and replaced them with fresh flowers. She tidied up her room of syringe caps, used gauze and other debris then kissed her. She walked over and opened her blinds and began to speak to Harmony as if she was lucid, which is what the Bishop suggested.

"Look sis, I've been crying long enough and you've been lying long enough. It's time to get up. I need for you to get up! I need for your heart to keep beating. I have nobody but you and I need you. Unfortunately, I'm all you got so GET UP! The security guard heard her yelling and popped his head in. "Everything alright in here?" He asked looking to see who Maya was yelling at. "I'm fine, just talking to my sister. Could you please leave us alone? Thanks." He pulled the door closed wondering if she'd lost her marbles.

"Harmony to be honest I don't feel guilty anymore. I'm feeling the same way all big sisters do! All older sisters worry about their siblings, even when you're doing well! We all become overprotective! We all give the best advice and try to keep you from things that could be potentially dangerous or have consequences! Frankly, I'm getting tired of always having to worry! I need you to GET UP!!! YOU HEAR ME? I NEED FOR YOU TO GET UP!!! God did not bring you this far to take you back! He's not finished! You're not finished!" Maya yelled passionately.

Just then, the door opened again. She swung her body around ready to firmly blast the security guard a final time when in stepped Gerald

McMillan, their father, standing in the doorway, formal dress gear holding his cello case. The room was silent. Maya's face was indicative of the shock and tension the trio held. He walked over pulled up a chair, took the cello out of the case and stood it in front of Maya.

Maya's face softened as she took the bow and began to play with all her heart. Surprisingly she didn't play a classical tune, a tune she'd normally play, or Gwen McMillan's favorite. Instead, she played *The Zone*, by an artist named The Weeknd, a song that Harmony would definitely have listened to herself.

Gerald offered no words. He strummed along on the bed rail complementing with percussion and both were pleased when they saw Harmony's heart monitor rising along with the beat! The colorful digital numbers on the display were fluctuating and rising, fluctuating and rising rhythmically!

The duet went on through the long song. Maya continued playing and blended the modern contemporary singer's sound right on into another great hit, *Earned It*, same artist. Harmony's fingers moved! Gerald banged the beat a little closer to his daughter's ear and her eyes darted back and forth then slowly opened. They continued to play with overwhelming tears in their eyes. Maya swung her bob and her vibrato increased as if she was playing for a great king of a foreign land long ago far away in Africa!

Miraculously, Harmony tilted her head and smiled softly as if being entertained by angels. Gerald grabbed Maya's forearm and she immediately ceased playing. She saw her sister smiling at her and yelled, "Security!!" The security guard sheepishly poked his head in. "Get the doctor!"

Chapter 10

While the physicians performed the necessary physiatric and psychological tests on Harmony, the nurses asked that the McMillans excuse themselves for the time being. They hesitantly obliged leaving together to have dinner in the hospital dining hall.

The estranged couple sat across from one another, each contemplating what to say. Where would one even begin? Each of them thinking of Harmony, not wanting to make this long awaited meeting about themselves, yet each knew there were a million unspoken moments that had passed. The history was all too intense, yet the present was to be celebrated.

Maya blew her French onion soup to cool it. She noticed Gerald avoided eye contact from the time he arrived and it was not missed by Maya. She desperately wanted to blurt out her feelings, but if it's one thing this taught her was to guard her heart and to be tactful. "Father I never realized how much Harmony favors you." Gerald looked down at his soup crumbling up the oyster crackers into it, "Gwen always said *you* look like me." He said. "You've grown up beautifully Maya, both of you have. I realize it wasn't easy without me, and you've done a great job with her. Ms. Takini, God rest her soul, did what I could not...not making excuses, just saying..."

Maya tossed her bob. "Father I don't blame you, not anymore. The Army separated us and forced me to take on tremendous responsibilities, but I have made my peace with it. I wouldn't have made the choices I've made if it weren't for your absence. I'm a stronger person because of it. I have too many friends with absent fathers that were neglectful for crazy reasons. I know why you had to be an Army lifer. I have no regrets."

"No regrets?" He said after listening intently finally making direct eye contact. "I decided to be a lifer to give you girls the best possible foundation. It wasn't solely a financial decision though. Maya, you have to know something. Gwen was the love of my life. I've never dated, never remarried. I have seen women casually but never anything serious. I left because I had some issues. You meet your soul mate once in a lifetime and if you're paying attention closely, and counting your blessings, God will allow you time. I knew that I wasn't in the right place after losing her, and I wasn't mentally prepared to let her go. If I had come home then, you'd probably have an alcoholic father who couldn't handle fatherhood. In retrospect, I, too, have no regrets."

That was all that need be said.

Maya considered his view without his love, but needed to discuss the miracle they just witnessed. "It was difficult watching Harmony outgrow most of her ailments after the transplant, and it didn't happen overnight. She had to return to Cooper month after month for years. After rejecting the 1st heart, I thought for sure her life was over. I thank God everyday for her. For years, I hated you for abandoning us, especially with her condition. I've written in my journal about you and all I was dealing with regarding her care. I don't think Ms. Takini ever had one night's full sleep. When Harmony's body began to thrive and we saw such a grand improvement, I encouraged her to live life to the fullest. She has dad. She really has. I wasn't prepared for God to take her this time, after preparing for it all of my life! Now is the time I need *her* the most. She's the stronger one after all."

Gerald empathized with Maya, "You two are strong in each other." Maya smiled then dabbed her mouth with the napkin. "What made you bring your cello?" She asked. "I'd gone by the loft to see you, but it's still taped off. Where have you been staying?" He asked. "I've been here. I haven't gone back home yet. Did anyone tell you any details of what happened? How did you find out?" She asked. Gerald perked up, "Detective Haynes and I went to school together. He requested the case."

Gerald and Maya talked and talked for hours. They laughed about some of Harmony's hijinks, her fun rap lyrics, her paragliding onto the Princeton Tiger's football field and her friends. They also talked about the prospect of having Gerald walk Maya down the aisle, when the time is right. They promised to have the deepest commitment at the start of their new beginning.

Most of all, they talked about Harmony's rough road ahead emotionally dealing with the fact that she and Keila Henson survived and the others did not, including Salope. Those friends were very dear to her, and Harmony's personality dictates that she will have survivor's remorse; she didn't get the chance to say goodbye, especially with Nyeem Jeffers. You never consider when you get dressed in the morning if it's going to be the last outfit you'll ever wear, and he was a clothes horse. Nyeem enjoyed life like Harmony did.

Gerald and Maya discussed how they would inform Harmony and also how to tell her that her attacker, who is still on the loose, went on this rampage because of Maya violating the rules of her position. "Don't beat yourself up." Gerald told her, "You were only letting Jack King know through your frame of reference and your experience with heart conditions, that he was not alone. Who knew out of desperation he would go to the lengths he has? He was from a big family you said. Some families don't talk.

You guys wouldn't have been able to talk me down from a ledge either. It is the condition of your heart that determines what we do to others. Jack King had a heart condition alright."

Maya understood. She felt absolutely guilt-free now, and was glad that their father had come. Gerald asked Maya, "When's the last time *you* had a good night's sleep?" Maya's eyes darted around the hall, "It's been about six weeks." She admitted. "I've only been to church and here." Gerald said, "Church is actually the hospital for sinners like us. Keep going it helps. It brings us closer to Him which is all He wants. Things happen to us that cause us to seek Him, but we really need to praise Him for what He does day by day."

They rose and hugged each other a good while, then made their way back to the elevators to see Harmony.

Chapter 11

Harmony McMillan was discharged from Capital Health and was admitted to Morris Hall two days after she came out of the coma. She didn't talk much, but Maya and Gerald managed to tell her everything about her attack and survival. Detective Haynes confirmed it all meeting with her after she moved in, and she filled him in on what happened to her from being chloroformed to hoisting herself backwards in the chair.

"I couldn't make out his face, but I remember his silhouette." Harmony whispered. "Maya saw his face; did she not tell you that? Detective Haynes asked. Harmony said, "Yes, she said she saw him looking down from the window she threw me out of. I've been thinking. If King was successful in getting my heart, what would he have done with it? He could have an accomplice. He could not have implanted it himself." Detective Haynes informed her, "If kept on ice, he could have taken it to Mexico, Canada,

Grenada, anywhere. Organs not only have been sold on the black market but doctors have been too. Whatever his intent, he committed murder to get it. You don't remember anything else he said? No previous interaction? It would help."

"I remember him saying he's been watching me, my routines, and there were times I felt uneasy at work, at the Smokehouse, at Jacque's too. I felt *watched*. He knew Maya wasn't coming home for a week and he also knew…" Detective Haynes interrupted, "No Harmony not what you inferred. What did you hear?"

Maya closed her eyes and thought about the sound of his voice. "He said, 'I'm doing what needs to be done…', and I asked what I could give that he felt he needed. He said, 'Your heart!'" Detective Haynes repeated her, "He said I'm doing what needs to be done…? Do you think he got cold feet?" Harmony shook her head, "Not a chance, he was all in! He was calculating and direct; no emotion and no yelling. He was so calm that I didn't see the punch coming, but up until then, he actually was not violent toward me, just cold and robotic. He was prepared to go all the way sir."

"I guess what I'm getting at Harmony is the fact that he only chloroformed you. Why didn't he kill you then? Why take the time to wait until you come to? What was his purpose of telling you his plan?" He asked. Harmony hadn't thought about it. He absolutely could have killed her, taken her heart and been halfway to Mexico before Maya got home. "I don't know." She admitted.

"You get your rest. I'll come back soon." He said.

Harmony slept for a couple hours then was awakened by an orderly to attend therapy. When she was returned by another, Maya was waiting for her. They discussed the angle Haynes brought up. "Maya this may be deeper than my heart. Since this happened, have you gone through Jack King's file at work? What has he been arrested for in the past? How much time did he serve?" Harmony asked.

"I have not. I've been here with you or at the church, but I am thoroughly familiar with Jack though. I saw him every week!" Maya said. "I know you do your job well, I'm not questioning that. I need you to look at it again." Harmony said, "...Whatever it is it's not going to jump out at you. It's going to be a bit abstract; subtle, know what I mean? See if you can view his medical file." Harmony said. "He's looking for motive? He said he wanted your heart! That ain't motive enough?!" Maya said. "I think this is deeper than we're looking sis. I realize that now." Harmony added.

Maya went to her office after hours and used her pass to enter. She clicked on her desk lamp and pulled the case of Jack King scanning through it seeing the same thing she'd always seen; Domestic Violence, Age 20, Dropped. Assault/Deadly Weapon, Age 24, Time Served. Aggravated Assault/Deadly Weapon, Age 29, Hung Jury/Acquitted, Battery, Age 34, Dropped. Aggravated Assault/Deadly Weapon, Age 41, Time Served. Attempted Robbery, Age 52, Time Served, Paroled G/B 2017. She viewed the aging mug shot photos.

When she went to return it to the file drawer she spotted a file lying horizontally between the hanging Pentaflex files and removed it. It was his medical history file.

Maya popped the large rubber band and began to fan through the ample physician's notes and lab reports. She didn't know exactly what she was looking for, but thought of her sister's words. She flipped each page scanning carefully until she got to the middle of the thick file and realized something she hadn't before. His blood type is O Negative. She and Harmony have AB Negative blood, the rarest form. 'Why...he wouldn't have been compatible for Harmony's heart at all' she thought, 'Detective Haynes made it clear that he was after her heart, but for whom?'

Maya read further into the documents in the file and was dumbstruck when she came upon a list of his diagnoses which read diabetes mellitus, sickle cell, mild hypertension, HIV, and Ileitis (Crohn's/colitis), Date of last exam: 12/24/16 just before his parole date.

Nothing in the file reflected he had a serious heart condition or heart disease. Nothing reflected he had been added to the heart transplant list. Nothing in the file reflected he had any issues with his heart EVER!

Maya was thoroughly confused. She sat mulling over it and thought about the hospital visit. The nurse did say he had a bad bout of angina. She again went back to his criminal file, checked his cellmates for each incarceration, his immediate family members, his wife and children and she saw something that registered. His wife suffered complications from a heart attack and is currently residing at Morris Hall!

Maya called Detective Haynes, "Sir Harmony's heart is not compatible for Jack King's blood type which is O Negative! I'm reading his file at my office. It's his wife's heart that's bad, not his! He intentionally missed his Parole meeting with me, don't you see!? He got admitted to Cooper under false pretenses, using angina to be admitted! He complained of chest tightening to get into the Cardiac Ward, but his true intent was to gain access to the records at the hospital! He's trying to save her life!!! Not his own!!! I'll bet you a million dollars she's low on that transplant list! She's at Morris Hall! He played on my emotions! He hasn't been stalking Harmony! He's been stalking US!!" Maya was out of breath, but she knew she was on the right track.

Detective Haynes tried to keep up, "Ms. McMillan, please slow down!"

"You have got to get over to the rehab! Please! She doesn't use King's name! She uses Deloro! Angela Deloro! He's there! Somewhere hiding! He probably hid when I was there! He's there just like he went right under my roof unnoticed! He may have changed his appearance! He's unassuming and elusive! He's in plain sight!"

Detective Haynes yelled, "Maya how could King know your sister would conk her head on your cello? It doesn't make any sense!" Maya yelled into the phone, "...Because *he* induced it!"

Chapter 12

Harmony McMillan flipped the remote on the rehab television looking for something good to watch. When she got bored with it she reached over to stick her ear buds in. The orderly tapped and walked into her room, "Time for your next test Ms. McMillan" he said moving the gurney closer to her offering assistance. Harmony snatched out one ear bud, "Again?" She asked accepting his hand to get onto the gurney. "Last one today. Promise." He said cheerfully.

The orderly pushed the gurney down the lighted corridor. He stopped, checked her IV bag, took out a syringe and stuck the point of the needle into the tube. Harmony knew from being in and out of hospitals that orderlies weren't supposed to do much more than transport, so she looked above her head at him. "What are you doing? What's the matter?" He smiled politely, "Just making sure it doesn't get tangled in the wheels. It does that sometimes."

Harmony began feeling sleepy and her eyes were getting heavy. "What...? Wh...Where?" She slurred. The orderly picked up the pace pushing the gurney and Harmony saw the silhouette she saw in her loft and knew it was him! She saw red and blue flashing lights and heard sirens, but could not react for the drug in her system. The rehab had a constant stream of emergency vehicles in and out all the time. She rolled over as far as she could and tried to yell for help, but he covered her face with the bed covers.

Jack King made a wild left turn racing with the gurney down several more corridors and out of the back of the facility! He wheeled the gurney onto the ramp of a waiting ambulance. Harmony tried to lift her head; she couldn't see clearly! "It's you...It's, stop, help!" She tried to say unsuccessfully, but onlookers knew this was an everyday occurrence. They probably figured he was doing what he always does. She wasn't loud enough for anyone to hear her and was feeling more sluggish by the minute.

He rolled her in alone. One of the staff doctors on a smoke break thought it odd that he didn't have assistance putting the gurney in and began walking over quickly when King jumped into the driver's seat of the EMT van. "Sir! Excuse me, Sir!" He said, but it peeled out leaving billows of tire smoke and burnt rubber aroma in the air. The doctor ran back through the back doors and encountered Detective Haynes questioning the nursing staff at the front desk. It was obvious that he was a cop in his long trench. He was speaking loudly and kept his hand on his waist holster revealing his badge and gun. "Harmony McMillan! I need to get to her room now!" He hollered.

The doctor yelled, "He...he went that way in an EMT van not even five minutes ago! He had a patient on a gurney! He peeled out!" He said walking briskly alongside telling the detective what he'd witnessed. Detective Haynes ran with him observing the tire tracks grabbing his radio blasting an All Points Bulletin and Be On The Look Out describing the vehicle. "Harmony McMillan's been kidnapped from Morris Hall!" He shouted. "She's in grave danger!" He ran back to the desk and shouted, "This building is officially a crime scene! Evacuate the building and notify me when Maya McMillan arrives!" He ran back to his car where Detective Cohen had heard the blast and was already speeding up to the front of the building. He jumped in and they sped off as the Lawrenceville Police Department pulled up, jumping out of their vehicles to cordon off the building. "We were too late!" He yelled. Detective Cohen drove like a bat out of hell in the direction the doctor pointed.

Meanwhile, Maya McMillan pulled up to the rehabilitation center and saw the scene. She got out of her car with her badge out, "Who's in charge?" She said with authority walking into the facility. One uniformed officer taping off the lobby said, "He's got her off the premises! Are you her sister?" He asked. "Yes! Where's Haynes?" She asked with haste. "He's on his trail! He got away in an ambulance!" Maya jumped in her car and grabbed her cell phone.

"For God's sake! Where are you?" She hollered into the phone. "I'm on #206 South! He's been spotted by Lawrence! They have him stopped and are approaching with weapons drawn! Maya listen! You have to let us bring him in, you understand?! You're too emotional...!" Haynes yelled, but Maya threw the phone and floored it!

When she saw the lights flashing, she slammed on her brakes and spun out jumping out of her car running toward Cohen who held the bullhorn. The scene was intense! The police from both jurisdictions approached the van cautiously on all sides and when one put his weapon into the window of it, a single gunshot could be heard. Maya gasped and stood still. They rushed the van pulling the driver's door open carefully. The body of Jack King slumped out.

Back at Morris Hall, the heavily guarded room of Angela Deloro netted truckloads of evidence hidden in her closet of Jack King's plan to implant Harmony's heart into her chest. Her laptop was forensically analyzed. King had researched heart surgery, infection, operating room procedures and defibrillator sales and he had extensively researched general anesthesia and coma meds. At the station, she was questioned for 22 hours, but it was clear she had no idea what he had planned. She informed them that she and Jack King were working on reconciliation, but he never let on his intent. Her official medical documentation revealed her blood type was AB Negative.

Maya and Harmony McMillan remained at the loft throughout their lives and never married. They respected their own privacy and each other's. Their father and brothers came to visit most holidays and their birthdays. Maya bought her sister a beautiful Shih Tzu she named Angel. Maya still works for the New Jersey Parole Office and Harmony remains on Disability, but works from home via online sales in antiquities. They live simply and quietly. Every day, Maya plays her bloodstained cello and Harmony writes in *her* journal. She threw away her ear buds, and they only listen to Christian music. They eat every meal together in their kitchen. The store and downstairs apartments remain vacant.

They attend services at St. Michael's Church on Warren Street and have dedicated their lives counting each day's blessing to Jesus Christ, their proclaimed Lord and Savior.

The End

About the Author

T E Williams is a married mother of 4 adult children born and raised in Trenton, New Jersey. A natural born writer, Mrs. Williams aspires to encourage people with thought-provoking works of fiction which celebrate avenues of adversity and stumbling blocks we all encounter. Her hope is to raise consciousness and to inspire readers from all backgrounds to avoid life's pitfalls and stay on the path laid out for you. She was inspired to write *Heart Condition* while remembering the lessons her parents' taught her about being aware of your surroundings. She hopes you will continue to support her in her effort to reach young people by reading *Twin Towers, After This, If Only, For Now & After All*. Mrs. Williams has also written *Flawless*, a Christian stage play for teens which was converted to paperback, and *You Can't Sit With Us!* Visit IreeSky.com to order. T E Williams is a Born-Again Christian and welcomes all audiences.

Made in the USA
Columbia, SC
05 November 2021

48068906R00059